TAIL OF TERROR

by John Sazaklis

illustrated by Patrycja Fabicka

PICTURE WINDOW BOOKS
a capstone imprint

Published by Picture Window Books,
an imprint of Capstone
1710 Roe Crest Drive
North Mankato, Minnesota 56003
capstonepub.com

Library of Congress Cataloging-in-Publication Data
Names: Sazaklis, John, author. | Fabicka, Patrycja, illustrator.
Title: Tail of terror / by John Sazaklis ; illustrated by Patrycja Fabicka
Description: North Mankato, Minnesota : Picture Window Books, an
imprint of Capstone., 2021. | Series: Boo books | Audience: Ages 5–7.
|Audience: Grades K–1. |
Summary: With his friends by his side and flashlight in hand, Mikey
investigates the old, haunted aquarium. Includes discussion questions,
writing prompts, and "scared silly" jokes.
Identifiers: LCCN 2021002497 (print) | LCCN 2021002498 (ebook) |
ISBN 9781663908834 (hardcover) | ISBN 9781663908841 (pdf) | ISBN
9781663908865 (kindle edition) Subjects: CYAC: Haunted places—
Fiction. | Aquariums—Fiction. | Horror stories.
Classification: LCC PZ7.S27587 Tai 2021 (print) | LCC PZ7.S27587
(ebook) | DDC [E]—dc23
LC record available at https://lccn.loc.gov/2021002497
LC ebook record available at https://lccn.loc.gov/2021002498

Design Elements: Shutterstock: ALEXEY GRIGOREV, vavectors, Zaie

Designer: Sarah Bennett

Printed and bound in the United States of America.   PO4270

TABLE OF
CONTENTS

CHAPTER ONE
THE OLD AQUARIUM

"There it is," Mikey said. "The old aquarium."

"You mean the haunted aquarium," said Jason. "People have heard a lot of spooky sounds coming from inside."

"I've heard about those noises,"

Mikey replied. "People say it's a

phantom or a ghost or something.

I don't believe it. Come on!"

He zoomed forward, leaving his

fearful friend no choice but to follow.

The front doors were locked shut with bolts and chains.

"Oh well. I guess we should just go home," Jason said.

"I'll find us another way in," said Mikey.

The friends went around to the back of the building.

"Man, it's really dark back here," Jason said.

"No problem," Mikey said, turning on his flashlight.

The back doors were bolted shut too.

Just then, a long, eerie moan filled the air.

OOOoooOOooOoOoooo!

Then a strange shadow appeared.
It loomed over them. In its grip was
a large hook!

Jason whirled around and
screamed.

"It's the phantom ghost thing!"
he cried.

The figure came closer and closer
to the two boys.

CHAPTER TWO

THE PHANTOM GHOST THING

"BOO!" it shouted. Then it began to laugh.

In the light, the boys saw a familiar face. It was not the phantom ghost thing. It was their friend Eve.

"Eve!" cried Mikey. "How did you know we were here?"

"Jason told me," she said. "And it looks like you could use my help."

She held up the hooked object in her hand. It was a crowbar.

Once again, a long, eerie moan filled the air.

OOOoooOOooOoOoooo!

"Do you hear that?" Jason asked.

"Of course I do!" Eve said.

"It's definitely the phantom ghost thing," Jason said, his voice shaking.

"It's not a phantom. It's not a ghost. This place is NOT haunted," Mikey said. "And I'm going to prove it."

He and Eve used the crowbar to open the door. A cold gust of wind blew out. *WHOOSH!*

Mikey led the way. The place reeked of salt water.

"There's something fishy going on," Eve joked.

Jason pinched his nose shut.

OOOOOOooooOOOOO!

This time the moan was louder.

And closer.

"There it is again!" Jason cried.

"This way!" shouted Mikey.

The three fearless friends reached
a dead end.

"We're trapped with the phantom
ghost thing!" shouted Jason.

"There's no such thing as a phantom ghost thing," Mikey said. "Right, Eve?"

"I'm not so sure anymore," she replied.

Mikey found a door and opened it. The kids slowly walked into an empty auditorium.

In the center was a huge pool. A full moon shined through the skylight.

The pool glowed bright blue. A large, black shape moved around inside. Mikey went to get a closer look. Eve and Jason followed.

CHAPTER THREE
KILLER TUNES

Suddenly, a wide-open mouth broke the pool's surface.

SPLASH!

Rows and rows of sharp teeth rushed at the kids.

The frightened friends were now dripping wet. The creature rested at the edge of the pool.

"That's no phantom ghost thing!" Mikey screamed. "It's a killer whale!"

"I prefer to be called an orca,"
said the whale. "It sounds nicer."

"You can talk?" Jason asked.

"Not only can I talk," she replied. "I can sing! I come here to practice every night. My voice bounces off the walls beautifully."

"Your voice is lovely," Eve added.

"Hello!" Mikey yelled. "You two are having a conversation with a talking killer whale! A. Killer. Whale! I'm out of here!"

Eve and Jason just laughed.

"Will you sing for us?" Eve asked.

"Yes. I'll perform songs from my favorite show," the whale said. "The Phantom of the Orca."

WHAAAA-OOOOO-UUUHHH!

AUTHOR

John Sazaklis is a *New York Times* bestselling author with almost 100 children's books under his utility belt! He has also illustrated Spider-Man books, created toys for *MAD* magazine, and written for the BEN 10 animated series. John lives in New York City with his superpowered wife and daughter.

ILLUSTRATOR

Patrycja Fabicka is an illustrator with a love for magic, nature, soft colors, and storytelling. Creating cute and colorful illustrations is something that warms her heart—even during cold winter nights. She hopes that her artwork will inspire children, as she was once inspired by *The Snow Queen, Cinderella,* and other fairy tales.

GLOSSARY

crowbar (KROH-bahr)—a tool made of iron that is shaped like a hook at one or both ends

eerie (EER-ee)—strange and frightening

figure (FIH-gyer)—a shape or form that looks like a body

gust (GUHST)—a sudden, strong blast of wind

loom (LOOM)—to show up in a great or enlarged form

reek (REEK)—a strong, unpleasant smell

whirl (WURL)—to turn around

DISCUSSION QUESTIONS

1. Do you believe in ghosts? Talk about your answer.

2. Was it safe for the kids to be sneaking into an old building? What would you have done?

3. How do you think the kids were feeling when they saw the orca? How would you feel?

WRITING PROMPTS

1. Some people think haunted houses are scary. Write about something that you think is scary.

2. Pretend you are the orca. Write a journal entry about meeting the kids.

3. The ending of this story is funny. Rewrite the ending to be scary instead.

SCARED SILLY JOKES!

Why are haunted houses so tall?
They have hundreds of horror stories!

What is a ghost's favorite drink?
ghoulade

What kind of TV is in a haunted house?
a big-scream TV

What is a ghost's favorite fruit?
booberries

What room does a ghost avoid?
the living room

What is a ghost's favorite dessert?
I-scream

What does a ghost do to stay safe in a car?
He puts on his sheet belt.

Why did the ghost cry?
She had a boo-boo.